HORRID HENRY'S DOUBLE DARE

Francesca Simon spent her childhood on the beach in California, and then went to Yale and Oxford Universities to study medieval history and literature. She now lives in London with her English husband and their son. When she is not writing books she is doing theatre and restaurant reviews or chasing after her Tibetan Spaniel, Shanti.

Tony Ross is one of Britain's best known illustrators, with many picture books to his name as well as line drawings for many fiction titles. He lives in Nottinghamshire.

GW00854446

Also by Francesca Simon

Don't Cook Cinderella
Helping Hercules

and for younger readers

Don't Be Horrid, Henry
Horrid Henry's Birthday Party

HORRID HENRY'S
DOUBLE DARE

Francesca Simon

Illustrated by Tony Ross

Orion
Children's Books

First published in Great Britain in 2009
by Orion Children's Books
a division of the Orion Publishing Group Ltd
Orion House
5 Upper St Martin's Lane
London WC2H 9EA
An Hachette UK company

1 3 5 7 9 10 8 6 4 2

Text © Francesca Simon 2009
Illustrations © Tony Ross 2009

The moral right of Francesca Simon and Tony Ross to be
identified as author and illustrator of this work has been asserted.

All rights reserved. No part of this publication may be
reproduced, stored in a retrieval system, or transmitted,
in any form or by any means, electronic, mechanical,
photocopying, recording or otherwise, without the prior
permission of Orion Children's Books.

A catalogue record for this book
is available from the British Library

Printed in Great Britain
by Clays Ltd, St Ives plc

ISBN 978 1 4440 0008 5

www.horridhenry.co.uk
www.orionbooks.co.uk

CONTENTS

THE PURPLE HAND RULES

The Purple Hand Club is the best
club ever. Naturally, everyone
wants to join. Well they can't. No
girls allowed and no wormy toad
little brothers - by order of me, the
Lord High Excellent Majesty of the
Purple Hand. Unless... Unless...
Well, maybe some people can EARN
their membership. They
have to be bold. They
have to be brave. And
most of all they have to
give me LOADS OF
SWEETS.

  We've got the scariest
dares and sneakiest
jokes - brilliant for
April Fool's Day,

or for tricking mean, horrible
parents, smelly crybaby brothers
and sisters, and bossy-boots girls
all year round. We also know all
the best jokes, tee hee!
P.S. Don't even bother reading
Frog-Face Margaret's copycat
book – it'll just make you
feel sick.

PETER: Henry, please
can I join your club?

NO WAY, WORM. Well,
okay, 'cause I'm so nice...

I DARE YOU TO:

• Sneak into Mum's
box of chocolates, pinch
her favourite Double
Chocolate Nutty Surprise and
bring it to me.

- Pretend to be helpful by making Dad a cup of tea and stir a teaspoon of salt into it instead of sugar.

- Stand outside in the street for an hour, holding a sign that says 'I AM A WORM'.

PETER: But everyone will laugh at me.

Too right, worm.

PETER: But I hate being laughed at.

Tough, you can't be in the Purple Hand Club. Why don't you go to

that old grouch face
Margaret's book. She
might let you join
her baby club.

Ha. He's gone.
Now I can tell you
my best little
brother jokes!

*Do you know why my little brother is built
upside down?*

Because his nose runs
and his feet smell!

PETER: Mum!
Henry said my
feet smell!

GET LOST!

How do you know if it's raining?
Push your little brother outside and see
if he comes in wet.

*Mum: Why won't you play
football with Peter?*
Henry: I'm bored of kicking him around.

*Dad: Don't be selfish, Henry. Let Peter use
the sledge half the time.*
Henry: I do, Dad. I use it going down
the hill and I let him use it coming up!

*Mummy Monster: What are you doing with
that saw and where's your little brother?*
Young Monster: He's only my half-
brother now! Ha ha!

*Miss Battle-Axe: Henry, if you had ten
sweets and Peter asked you for one, how
many sweets would you have then?*
Henry: Ten!

PETER: Your jokes are horrid, Henry.

No, they aren't. Henry rules!

MORE OF HENRY'S HORRIBLE TRICKS

• If your little brother or sister is watching TV and you want to watch something really great, like *Rapper Zapper* or *Gross-Out*, tell them that Mum and Dad want to see them — urgently. As soon as they're out of the room, grab the remote!

• Tell your mum that your little brother or sister has been scratching their head all day. Your mum will think they've got nits — and send to them to the Nit Nurse, or torture them with the nit comb for hours. Tee hee.

• Hide your mum or dad's glasses or car keys. When they've searched everywhere, pretend to find them. Your mum and dad will think you are very clever and let you watch TV all night, or give you loads of sweets as a reward.

• Hold a jumble sale and put your little brother or sister up for sale. Warning: you might not get paid very much money but it's better than having them bug you all day.

• Take your dad's favourite CD out of its case and replace it with something really good of your own. Watch while he relaxes in his chair, ready to listen to his boring old CD and the Killer Boy Rats boom out!

RUDE RALPH'S REVOLTING TRICKS, JOKES AND DARES

Hey Ralph, I bet you know some super-rude tricks and jokes, guaranteed to make all prissy toads run away screaming.

RALPH: Yeah, how about these really revolting dares?

RALPH'S RUDE AND REVOLTING DARES

- Dare your friend to kiss four bare legs and a bare bottom. (All this really means is that they have to kiss a chair, but don't tell them that!)

- Dare a prissy girl to smell the feet of everyone in the room and put them in order from best to worst.

Bet mine are the BEST. They smell like the stinkiest cheese ever.

- During school dinner, shout out something stupid, like 'I LOVE MY TEACHER!'

- Tell a very rude joke to your teacher. Teachers love rude jokes.

YEAH! Go Ralph!

RALPH'S RUDE JOKES

Who shouted 'knickers' at the Big Bad Wolf?
Little Rude Riding Hood.

What did the traffic lights say to the car?
Don't look at me, I'm changing.

What do you get if you cross
a skunk with a dinosaur?
A stinkasaurus.

What do you call an elephant that never
washes?
A smellyphant.

What flies through the air and stinks?
A smelly-copter.

What do you do if you
find a python in your
toilet?
Wait until he's finished.

What happens when
the queen burps?
She issues a royal
pardon.

MOODY MARGARET: We don't want nappy-face Peter in our club either.

RUDE RALPH: Hey Peter, if you give me your pocket money, I'll make Henry let you join the Purple Hand Club.

RUDE RALPH'S POCKET MONEY PRANKS

RUDE RALPH: If you've got some money buy a whoopee cushion and some magic soot. They'll be your best buys ever.

- Use the whoopee cushion at home when your mum and dad have some important guests round for dinner. Everyone will really enjoy your trick because it'll liven up their boring evening.

- Sprinkle the magic soot on your living room carpet. This joke works best when your carpet has just been hoovered!

NEW NICK'S TASKS

RUDE RALPH: Hey Henry, Nick wants to join the Purple Hand Club.

No way! Wait a minute, what if he's got loads of sweets to give us. Let's give him three tasks to do and if he succeeds, we'll let him join.

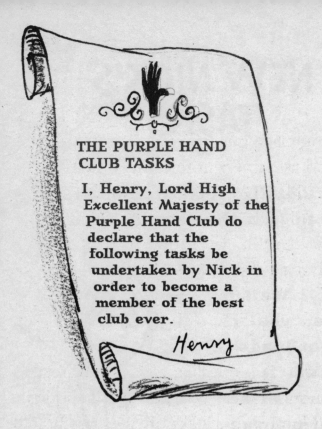

**THE PURPLE HAND
CLUB TASKS**

**I, Henry, Lord High
Excellent Majesty of the
Purple Hand Club do
declare that the
following tasks be
undertaken by Nick in
order to become a
member of the best
club ever.**

Henry

1. Before Miss Battle-Axe enters the classroom in the morning, sneak a plastic spider on her chair. You will only pass this task if (a) nobody spots you with the spider, and (b) Miss Battle-Axe runs out of the room screaming!

**MOODY MARGARET:
I'm going to tell on you!**

2. During class, put up your hand and ask a very interesting question, like, 'Do you like peanut butter sandwiches?' or 'Did Queen Victoria ever ask you round to tea?' You will only pass this task if Miss Battle-Axe looks at you as though you are a total worm and gets VERY angry.

3. At lunchtime, complain to Greasy Greta, the Demon Dinner Lady, that the custard is cold and lumpy. You will only pass this task if you still manage to get some dinner!

LATER…

NEW NICK: I've done all three tasks. Can I be in the Purple Hand Club now?

Got any sweets?

NEW NICK: Loads!
Just not on me.

No sweets, eh? The penalty is...

THREE MORE PURPLE HAND CLUB TASKS

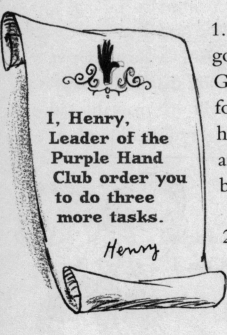

I, Henry, Leader of the Purple Hand Club order you to do three more tasks.

Henry

1. Swap one of the goodies in Greedy Graham's lunchbox for something healthy from yours — and scoff it up before he finds out.

2. Muddle up two people's names, and call them the wrong names all day.

The two people have to be — Margaret and Susan.

3. Write a fake love letter from Gorgeous Gurinder to Beefy Bert.

To my Handsome Bert

Lovely Bert
You are as beefy
as can be
Would you like
To come to tea?

Gurinder xx

RUDE RALPH:
Nice one, Henry!

LATER…

NEW NICK: I've done all three tasks. Can I join the Purple Hand Club now?

Nearly - just one more totally gross task…

TOTALLY GROSS PURPLE HAND CLUB TASK

Go over to Margaret's house and offer to play school with her. That bossy-boots grouch is always the teacher and the head and you have to be the teacher's pet. Ha ha!

RUDE RALPH: Oh no! He won't do that even to be in the Purple Hand!

LATER...

NEW NICK: I've done the totally gross task. Now, can I be in the Purple Hand Club?

HORRID HENRY AND RUDE RALPH: We'll think about it.

GREEDY GRAHAM'S FOOD FUN

Graham always has loads of sweets. He'd be a brilliant member of the Purple Hand Club. Graham, do you know any good dares?

GREEDY GRAHAM'S DARES

- Eat a chocolate bar using a knife and fork.

Not fair!

- Eat a whole doughnut without licking your lips once.

- Eat an apple in just ten bites. You can leave the stalk and core if you want.

Apples - yeuch!

- Eat a muffin without using your hands.

FOOD FIGHTS

- Find out who can fit the most marshmallows in their mouth at once.

- Float some apples in a bucket of water, and see who can fish the most out with their mouth.

Not more apples! Gross!

- Find out who can eat the most cream crackers in one minute, without having a drink of water.

Are all your dares about food?

- Move twenty chocolates from one plate to another using a straw. Race with a friend to see who can do it the quickest.

GREEDY GRAHAM: Hint - you could always eat the chocolates afterwards!

* Talk about cucumbers for thirty seconds, without saying 'um' or 'er'.

That's easy-peasy! Cucumbers are gross and green and ... um ... er ...

GREEDY GRAHAM: Here's one for you, Henry. Stand with your back against a wall, with your feet together and the backs of your heels touching the wall. I'll put this chocolate bar about thirty centimetres

in front of you. Now try to pick
up the chocolate without moving
your feet or bending your knees.
I bet you can't do it without
falling over.

That's not fair! It's impossible!
Forget the dares, tell us some
jokes.

GREEDY GRAHAM'S JOKES

Waiter, do you serve fish?
Sit down, sir, we serve anybody.

*Brainy Brian: Miss Battle-Axe, I've got a
bone stuck in my throat.*
Miss Battle-Axe: Are you choking?
Brainy Brian: No, I'm serious.

Waiter, this egg is bad.
Don't blame me, I only laid the table.

Waiter, will my pizza be long?
No, sir, it'll be round.

*How do you stop someone
stealing fast food?*
Fit a burger alarm.

What did the teddy say when
he was offered pudding?
No, thanks, I'm stuffed.

Why do tigers eat raw meat?
Because they can't cook.

Why do the French like to eat snails?
Because they don't like fast food!

**So you've
eaten at
Restaurant Le
Posh too!**

AEROBIC AL'S ATHLETIC DARES AND JOKES

AEROBIC AL: I know a lot of great dares and I dare you to try them. If you practise every day you might get to be almost as good as me!

- Balance a cup of water on your head and throw a ball into a hula hoop – at the same time.

AEROBIC AL: I won a medal for being best at this.

- Jump on one leg for twenty seconds with both hands on your head.

AEROBIC AL: I can do this for much longer than twenty seconds, but I thought I'd better make it easy for you.

- Do twenty star jumps, singing nursery rhymes at the same time.

- Balance a ball on a tennis racket and walk down the street.

These dares are as bad as PE at school! We don't do stuff like that in the Purple Hand Club – we watch loads of TV and scoff crisps and sweets.

AEROBIC AL: What about these fun dares then?

AEROBIC AL'S DARING DARES

- When you're at the swimming pool, shout, 'Look out for the shark!' then quickly leap out of the pool.
- Knock on your neighbour's front door and run away very fast.

That's more like it. Especially since Frog-Face Margaret is my next-door-neighbour. Tee hee!

- Kick as many footballs as you can over your next-door-neighbour's fence before they spot you.

Even better if you accidentally on purpose make one land on their head.

AEROBIC AL: I know some good sporty jokes too.

AEROBIC AL'S SPORTY JOKES

Why are bananas good at gymnastics?
Because they're great at doing the splits.

Why can't you play sports in the jungle?
Because of all the cheetahs.

*Why did the golfer wear two
pairs of pants?*
In case he got a
hole-in-one!

What's a waiter's best sport?
Tennis, because he is good at serving.

What has twenty-two legs and goes, 'Crunch, crunch, crunch'?
A football team eating crisps.

What do runners do when they forget something?
They jog their memories!

HORRID HENRY'S MONEY-MAKING SCHEMES

RUDE RALPH: What did you get for Christmas, Henry?

A drumkit. It's the best present I've ever had.

RUDE RALPH: Why?

My mum pays me not to play it!

HORRID HENRY'S MARVELLOUS MONEY-MAKING IDEAS

 Offer to sell Moody Margaret's Secret Club password to anyone who'll pay a pound.

PERFECT PETER: I know Margaret's Secret Club password, and I know the Purple Hand password too. It's...

We've changed the password. Nah nah ne nah nah. Go back to the girls' book, slimy toad.

PERFECT PETER: Mum! Henry called me a slimy toad!

MUM: Henry! Don't be horrid!

Set up a stall and sell all your old baby toys at top prices. Help yourself to your wormy worm brother's good toys. He's got far too many.

Tell your parents that you're going to be perfect for a whole day — but only if they pay.

PERFECT PETER: That's not fair. I'm always perfect, and they don't pay me.

Get lost, toady toad.

Offer to do the hoovering for your mum if she pays you. When she's out of the room, turn on the hoover, then settle down in a comfy chair with your favourite comic.

Hide the TV remote control. Suggest to your parents that they pay a pound to whoever finds it. Then — yippee! — it just happens to be you.

Get your mum to pay you for eating all your vegetables. She'll be so delighted you're going to eat healthily that she'll agree. Then, at tea time, when no one's looking, sneak the vegetables under the table, into your pockets and later into the bin.

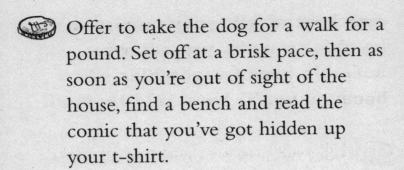 Offer to take the dog for a walk for a pound. Set off at a brisk pace, then as soon as you're out of sight of the house, find a bench and read the comic that you've got hidden up your t-shirt.

 Collect all the fruit and vegetables from your kitchen and set up a stall outside your house, with a poster reading – 'Home-Grown Organic Fruit and Veg'.

And best of all, your mum won't
be able to make you eat any
horrible green vegetables –
because you'll have sold them all.

 Tell your friends that you can make
coins vanish. When they hand over
their money, sneak it into your
pockets, then shout, 'Abracadabra! It's
magic – your money has vanished!'
When they ask you to make it
reappear, just say you haven't learned
that part of the trick yet.

BEEFY BERT GETS BAMBOOZLED

Bert, do you know any good tricks or dares?

BEEFY BERT: I dunno.

Do you know any good jokes?

BEEFY BERT: I dunno.

I'd better tell you my jokes then.

HORRID HENRY'S JOKES

How do you baffle Beefy Bert?
Put him in a round room and tell him
to sit in the corner.

What did Beefy Bert call his zebra?
Spot.

How do you catch a squirrel?
Climb up a tree and act like a nut.

**MOODY MARGARET :
Don't even think you
can join the Secret
Club, Bert. You need to
be clever to be a member
of my club.**

**He doesn't want to join your
girly club, do you, Bert?**

BEEFY BERT: I dunno.

MORE DARES FOR BEEFY BERT

- Run around wearing socks on your hands, trousers for a shirt and a shirt for trousers for three minutes.

- Sing 'I'm a little Teapot' and do all the actions.

- Stick out your tongue and touch your nose.

PSST! I never said you had to touch your nose with your tongue. Ha ha. You can stick out your tongue – and touch your nose with a finger!

BEEFY BERT: ??!!??

A BUZZING BALLOON TRICK TO BAFFLE BEEFY BERT

Here's a trick to keep Beefy Bert baffled for hours:

- Blow up a balloon, but don't tie up the end.

- Place the end of the balloon between the door and the doorframe and close the door quickly to hold the balloon.

- When Bert opens the door, the balloon will whiz all over the room — and Bert won't have any idea where it's come from!

RUDE RALPH'S RUDEST JOKES EVER

RUDE RALPH: I'll beat the stupid girls' club easily with my rude and rotten jokes.

MOODY MARGARET: Oh no, you won't.

RUDE RALPH: Bet I will.

MOODY MARGARET: Go on then. I dare you.

First man: My dog's got no nose.
Second man: How does he smell?
First man: Awful.

MOODY MARGARET: Boo!

Why do girls wear make-up and perfume?
Because they're ugly and they smell.

MOODY MARGARET: I think you mean that BOYS are ugly and smelly!

RUDE RALPH: Margaret eats like a bird.
HORRID HENRY: You mean she hardly eats a thing?
RUDE RALPH: No, she eats slugs and worms.

MOODY MARGARET: NO, I DON'T!

Have you heard about Margaret? She isn't pretty and she isn't ugly.
She's pretty ugly!

MOODY MARGARET: HA HA HA. Not!

What do you call a girl with a carrot stuck in each ear?
Anything, she can't hear you.

NEW NICK'S FINAL TASKS

MOODY MARGARET: Nick is really nice. He's not horrible and smelly like the Purple Hand Club. Nick, you can be in the Secret Club if you want.

NEW NICK: Oh no! Not the girls' club! Please let me in the Purple Hand. I'll do anything you ask.

THREE MORE TERRIBLE TASKS FOR NICK BY ORDER OF THE PURPLE HAND LEADER

Henry

1. Wear a pair of girl's knickers to school and get through the day without anyone finding out.

2. Tell us some good jokes.

NEW NICK'S JOKES

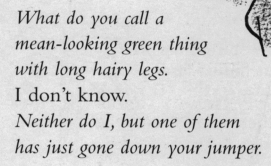

What kind of dog smells of onions?
A hot dog.

What do you call a mean-looking green thing with long hairy legs.
I don't know.
Neither do I, but one of them has just gone down your jumper.

What's yellow on the inside and green on the outside?
A banana dressed up as a cucumber.

What lies in a pram and wobbles?
A jellybaby.

What do you call a sleeping bull?
A bulldozer.

How do you describe a lazy skeleton?
Bone idle.

3. Go over to Moody Margaret's book and give her a bunch of flowers. But hide a fat juicy worm inside them! Tee hee!

NEW NICK: Done it. You should have heard Margaret scream when the worm leaped out at her.

MOODY MARGARET: You disgusting frogface! I HATE YOU!

NEW NICK: Mission accomplished. And I've got a bag of Big Boppers, some fizzywizz drinks and lots of gumballs.

HENRY AND RALPH: Welcome to the Purple Hand Club!

THE PURPLE HAND RULES OK!

Purple Hand rules OK! We've got all the best dares and all the best jokes.

MOODY MARGARET: That's rubbish! If you want to find out what a proper dare is come on over to my book...

No more Mr Nice Guy! This time it's war. On guard, Margaret. The Purple Hand has dares for all of the Secret Club and any other gruesome girls. If you fail, Purple Hand wins.

LAZY LINDA has to run down the street in her pyjamas – in the morning.

CLEVER CLARE has to get all her spellings wrong in the next spelling test.

SINGING SORAYA has to go through a whole day without singing a note.

GORGEOUS GURINDER has to wear Perfect Peter's clothes all day.

FIERY FIONA has to spend an hour not getting angry or annoyed once.

SOUR SUSAN has to smile sweetly for a whole day.

You're going to lose. You're going to lose. Nah na ne nah nah.

MOODY MARGARET: What's my dare then? Bet you can't think of anything I can't do better than anyone else.

I dare you to let me be Captain Hook next time we play pirates and not moan about it.

MOODY MARGARET: Let you play with my hook? No way! Walk the plank, you pongy pants pimple.

The enemy has retreated! The Purple Hand triumphs again. My club's the best, and my book's the best too. Read on for the offical, top secret results . . .

Top Secret Results

	SECRET CLUB	PURPLE HAND
Dares/Tricks	-5,000	80,000
Jokes	-10,000	1,000,000

RESULT: The Secret Club loses. **Purple Hand is the BEST!** Now it's your turn to award points for the dares, tricks and jokes in this book:

DARES/TRICKS	...../10
JOKES	...../10
GRAND TOTAL	...../20

When you've read *Moody Margaret Strikes Back*, fill in your score for that book too. Which book came out on top?

HORRID HENRY'S DOUBLE DARES	...../20
MOODY MARGARET STRIKES BACK	...../20

HORRID HENRY BOOKS

Horrid Henry
Horrid Henry and the Secret Club
Horrid Henry Tricks the Tooth Fairy
Horrid Henry's Nits
Horrid Henry Gets Rich Quick
Horrid Henry's Haunted House
Horrid Henry and the Mummy's Curse
Horrid Henry's Revenge
Horrid Henry and the Bogey Babysitter
Horrid Henry's Stinkbomb
Horrid Henry's Underpants
Horrid Henry Meets the Queen
Horrid Henry and the Mega-Mean Time Machine
Horrid Henry and the Football Fiend
Horrid Henry's Christmas Cracker
Horrid Henry and the Abominable Snowman
Horrid Henry Robs the Bank

Horrid Henry's Big Bad Book
Horrid Henry's Wicked Ways
Horrid Henry's Evil Enemies
Horrid Henry Rules the World
Horrid Henry's House of Horrors

Horrid Henry's Joke Book
Horrid Henry's Jolly Joke Book
Horrid Henry's Mighty Joke Book

Visit Horrid Henry's website at
www.horridhenry.co.uk for competitions, games,
downloads and a monthly newsletter!

MOODY MARGARET STRIKES BACK

Francesca Simon spent her childhood on the beach in California, and then went to Yale and Oxford Universities to study medieval history and literature. She now lives in London with her English husband and their son. When she is not writing books she is doing theatre and restaurant reviews or chasing after her Tibetan Spaniel, Shanti.

Tony Ross is one of Britain's best known illustrators, with many picture books to his name as well as line drawings for many fiction titles. He lives in Nottinghamshire.

Complete list of Horrid Henry
titles at the end of the book

Also by Francesca Simon

Don't Cook Cinderella
Helping Hercules

and for younger readers

Don't Be Horrid, Henry
Horrid Henry's Birthday Party

MOODY MARGARET STRIKES BACK

Francesca Simon

Illustrated by Tony Ross

Orion
Children's Books

First published in Great Britain in 2009
by Orion Children's Books
a division of the Orion Publishing Group Ltd
Orion House
5 Upper St Martin's Lane
London WC2H 9EA
An Hachette UK company

1 3 5 7 9 10 8 6 4 2

Text © Francesca Simon 2009
Illustrations © Tony Ross 2009

The moral right of Francesca Simon and Tony Ross to be
identified as author and illustrator of this work has been asserted.

All rights reserved. No part of this publication may be
reproduced, stored in a retrieval system, or transmitted,
in any form or by any means, electronic, mechanical,
photocopying, recording or otherwise, without the prior
permission of Orion Children's Books.

A catalogue record for this book
is available from the British Library

Printed in Great Britain
by Clays Ltd, St Ives plc

ISBN 978 1 4440 0009 2

www.horridhenry.co.uk
www.orionbooks.co.uk

CONTENTS

MOODY MARGARET'S SECRET CLUB

Naturally the Secret Club is the best club ever. I'm the boss, everyone does what I say, and there are no boys allowed. Henry and his stinky Purple Hand Club are always planning stupid tricks and dares or telling their UNfunny jokes, but we can outdo the boys any day. After all we're the ones who stinkbombed the Purple Hand and spiked their drinks and booby-trapped their entrance

1

and even stole their
entire fort. HA!

HORRID HENRY:
Margaret doesn't know
any good jokes, tricks
or dares. Don't read her book –
mine's much better!

Boys' jokes are NOT funny, but
my jokes ABOUT boys definitely
are.

*What's the difference between
a boy and a cowpat?*
A cowpat stops
being smelly after a
couple of days.

*Why did the boy take a
pencil to bed?*
To draw the curtains.

2

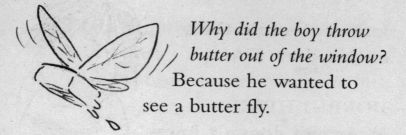

Why did the boy throw butter out of the window? Because he wanted to see a butter fly.

Rude Ralph made a rude noise in class. 'Stop that!' said Miss Battle-Axe.
'OK,' said Rude Ralph. 'Which way did it go?'

Doctor Dettol: Is your cough any better now?
Henry: It's much better, thank you. I've been practising for weeks.

Hey! Susan! You lazy lump! You're meant to be on the look-out. I just saw Henry sneaking around trying to spy on us.

SOUR SUSAN: I saw him. I am NOT a lazy lump!

I think that pongy pimple and his stupid club are up to something – and we need to find out what...

AN ENEMY
IN THE CAMP

Halt!
Who
goes
there?

SOUR
SUSAN:
It's the enemy. Send him back to
Henry's book.

PERFECT PETER: Can't I be in
your club? Henry is being horrid
to me. He won't let me join the
Purple Hand.

I don't want that little worm in
my club.

SOUR SUSAN: But maybe we could use him to spy on the Purple Hand.

I was just about to say that before you did.

SOUR SUSAN: Bossyboots.

Okay, Peter, we'll let you be in our club, if you tell us all your best tricks to outwit Henry.

PERFECT PETER'S TRICKS TO OUTWIT HENRY

- At night, wait until everyone's asleep, then creep downstairs and sleep there so you can take control of the TV remote first thing in the morning.

- Mess up Henry's room even more so that mine looks tidier than ever, Mum and Dad will reward me with extra pocket money, and punish Henry with no TV and no sweets for a week.

- Wrap up a piece of carrot in a  chocolate wrapper and leave it lying in the kitchen. Just watch Henry's face when he grabs the 'chocolate bar' and rips off the wrapper.

- Put blue food colouring in water or milk so that Henry will think it's a nasty, sweet drink and guzzle it all up.

- Ask Henry if you can test some new chocolate on him. Blindfold him and say, 'Open your mouth, and I'll pop it in.' When Henry is sitting with his mouth wide open, feed him a spoonful of prune yogurt.

Peter, now creep over to Henry's book, and find out what tricks he's planning to play on us.

SECOND IN COMMAND

When Peter comes back, let's give him some dares to do. Ha ha. Do you know any good ones?

SOUR SUSAN: If I tell you, will you promise to make me your Second in Command?

We'll see how good they are.

SOUR SUSAN'S DARES FOR PERFECT PETER

- Tell the bogey babysitter there's a creepy-crawly in her hair or climbing up her back. Watch her wriggle and scream!

- Put Henry's alarm on for four in the morning.

- If the babysitter sends you to bed too early, hide the remote, so that she can't watch TV all evening. Serves her right. Nah nah ne nah nah.

- In the middle of story time with Miss Lovely at school, give your best and loudest snort.

- Suck a slice of sour lemon, then try to whistle.

- When you've settled down to watch your favourite TV programme, *Manners with Maggie*, remove the batteries from the remote control so that Henry can't change channels to *Mutant Max*.

- While blindfolded feel a volunteer's face and see if you can guess who it is.

We can have loads of fun with that one. I'll blindfold Peter, and we'll get him to feel your face. Then while he's sitting there trying to think who it could be, we'll run off and hide.

- Eat a bowlful of Glop.

SOUR SUSAN: Am I Second in Command now?

Mmm, I might let Linda be Second. You can be Third. Unless you know any good jokes.

SOUR SUSAN'S JOKES

What do you call an insect who is always complaining?
A grumble bee.

How did the jockey talk to his pony?
In a hoarse voice.

Why won't oysters share?
Because they are shellfish.

Why are adults always complaining?
Because they are groan ups.

My mum lets me watch the TV all day.
Wow, I wish she was my mum.
No, you don't. She won't let me turn it on.

**Oh, go on then. You can be
Second in Command.**

NEW BEST FRIEND

Gurinder, do you want to be in my Secret Club?

GORGEOUS GURINDER: I don't know. I might join the Purple Hand Club instead. What's so good about the secret club?

We know all the best jokes and dares. Listen to these...

MORE OF MOODY MARGARET'S JOKES

Boy: I have three noses, five eyes and four mouths. What am I?
Girl: Very ugly.

Why was the boy upset when he won the prize for the scariest disguise at the Halloween party?
Because he only came to pick up his little sister!

Miss Battle-Axe: Henry, you scruffy boy, you've got holes in your trousers.
Henry: Of course I have. It's so I can get my legs in them!

Did you hear about the boy who put on a clean pair of socks every day?
By the end of the week he couldn't get his shoes on!

Miss Battle-Axe: Henry, if you had five pounds in one pocket and three pounds in another pocket, what would you have?
Horrid Henry: Someone else's trousers on.

Gurinder, you're a lot nicer than Susan and not so sour. If you join the Secret Club, you can be Second in Command if you like. And you can be my new best friend and come to my home for a sleepover.

SOUR SUSAN: Can I come?

No, you're not invited

SOUR SUSAN: That's not fair. She has got to do some dares first.

All right. You think up some good dares then.

SOUR SUSAN: Don't worry I will. You mean bossyboots.

What did you say?

SOUR SUSAN: Nothing (grouch).

SOUR SUSAN'S SLEEPOVER DARES FOR MOODY MARGARET

- Tie Gurinder's hair up in a silly-looking style, and make her keep it like that all the next day.

- Give Gurinder an amazing make-over, wearing a blindfold.

- Wait until Gurinder's asleep, then draw on her face with soap crayons or face paints and take some photographs to shock her with later.

- Mummify Gurinder using toilet paper.

- Scream in the middle of the night and wake her up.

SOUR SUSAN: Ha ha! Gurinder won't be Margaret's new best friend for long.

18

PERFECT PETER:
Margaret, I've got a
secret to tell you.
It's…

Go away, worm! Tell
me later. I'm busy.

19

MOODY MARGARET'S TOP TRICKS

Susan's dares are so mean, but they're still loads better than any of the boys' dares.

HORRID HENRY: You're wrong. Boys are best!

You won't be saying that when you've heard my top tricks.

MOODY MARGARET'S TOP TRICKS

- Tell all the boys Nurse Needle will be at school because it's injection day. Then sit back and watch Tough Toby tremble and Weepy William wail!

SOUR SUSAN: Henry's the worst. He's a great big crybaby.

I'll pretend to feel sorry for them - with my trick tissue box.

- Take out the top ten tissues from a tissue box, and sellotape them together. Do this by taking the bottom edge of one tissue and gluing it to the top edge of another tissue, until you've done them all. Then put them back in the

21

box carefully, so that no one can tell there's anything odd about them. When one of the boys starts crying because he thinks Nurse Needle is coming, offer him a tissue – and make him look like a complete fool!

Ha ha! Here are some more tricks to get my own back on Henry.

• Knock on your next-door-neighbour's door, smile sweetly and tell them that your pet snake or tarantula is loose in their garden.

In my case, this means Henry.

- Hide Horrid Henry's favourite toy, Mr Kill. He can't sleep without it!

- Thread a piece of fine cotton through a five pound note, and place the note on the floor. When Henry sees it and tries to pick it up, pull the cotton away from him!

- When playing Henry's favourite board game, Gotcha, with him, make sure that you're the banker – and pinch lots of treasure from the bank when Henry's not looking. Then he'll be a loser every time!

HORRID HENRY:
Margaret, Susan –
I've got a dare
for you.

HENRY'S DARE

- Don't laugh, giggle or even smile for
  one whole minute while everyone else
  tells you jokes and pulls funny faces.

**MOODY MARGARET AND SOUR
SUSAN: BAH! That is SO EASY!**

**Here's Clare. She'd make a great
Second in Command. She's
cleverer than Susan, and she'll
know how to outwit Henry.**

CLEVER CLARE'S TRICKS, JOKES AND DARES

CLEVER CLARE:
Do you want to
know some brilliant
ways to make some
money out of Henry?

**MOODY MARGARET
AND SOUR SUSAN:**
Yes please!

PERFECT PETER:
Shall I tell
you the
secret now?

Not now. I told you to go
away.

HOW CLEVER CLARE TRICKS MONEY OUT OF HORRID HENRY

Dare Henry to say the alphabet backwards. If he can, you have to give him a pound. But if he gets it wrong, he has to give you a pound.

CLEVER CLARE: I think I can safely say that Henry will be handing over a pound.

Say to Henry: 'I dare you to write with your toes on a piece of a paper.' Tell him that if he can do it, you'll give him a pound. If not, he owes you. When he's struggled unsuccessfully for a few minutes, produce another piece of paper that you prepared earlier. On the paper you have written 'with your toes'.

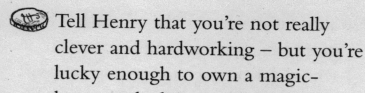 Tell Henry that you're not really clever and hardworking – but you're lucky enough to own a magic-homework-doing-pencil. Trick Henry into buying the pencil from you, and see how long it takes him to realise it's just an ordinary pencil.

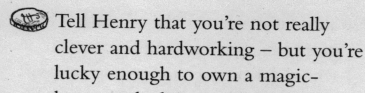 Offer to do Henry's homework for him – for a pound. But do it all wrong so that he still gets a rotten mark.

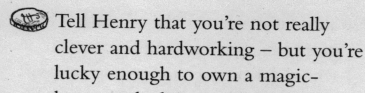 Write Henry a fake sick note from his mum for school:

Dear Miss Battle-Axe

Henry is ill, and will not be at school today.

Henry's Mum

Show it to Henry and tell him if he gives you a pound, you'll take it to school for him. Then quickly make a few changes!

Dear Miss Battle-Axe

Henry is *pretending to be* ill, but he will ~~not~~ be at school today.
still

Henry's Mum

Henry's going to be in such trouble at school. Nah nah ne nah nah!

CLARE'S CLEVEREST JOKES

What goes zzub zzub?
A bee flying backwards.

*What's bright orange and sounds
like a parrot?*
A carrot.

How do you make a pirate angry?
Take away the 'p' and he becomes irate.

*A frog went into a library. The librarian,
trying to be kind, offered it all sorts of books
to read.*
But the sulky frog didn't want any of
them – it just sat there saying 'reddit,
reddit, reddit.'

What do snakes learn at school?
Hiss–tory.

CLEVER CLARE'S FAVOURITE BOOKS

Easy Money by Robin Banks
Cliff Tragedy by Eileen Dover
The Hole in my Bucket by Lee King
Hungry Dog by Nora Bone
The Long Walk to School by Mr Bus

CLEVER CLARE'S RIDDLES

What has teeth but cannot eat?
A comb.

What gets wet the more it dries?
A towel.

What word is always spelled incorrectly?
Incorrectly.

*How many apples can you put in
an empty box?*
One. After that it's not empty any more.

CLEVER CLARE'S CLEVEREST TRICK

When your mum and dad have finished with their newspaper, hide it in your bedroom. When next morning's paper is delivered, sneakily swap the insides with yesterday's, leaving only the new front page. Watch to see if your parents notice that they are reading yesterday's news all over again!

You're so clever, Clare! You can be my Second in Command, if you like.

FIERY FIONA'S FUN

There's Fiona. Let's wind her up with some annoying tricks and jokes.

CLEVER CLARE: But let's tell her that they're all Henry's ideas. Then she'll be mad at him instead of us.

Good thinking. Hey Fiona, listen to Henry's jokes. I think he's trying to annoy you.

JOKES TO FIRE UP FIERY FIONA

What's Fiery Fiona's favourite food?
Scream cakes.

Why does Fiery Fiona ban whispering?
Because it's not aloud.

What kind of puzzle makes Fiery Fiona angry?
A crossword.

Knock knock
Who's there?
Boo
Boo who?
Don't cry, Fiona, it's only a joke.

FIERY FIONA:
Ha ha. Henry's
so horrible.

He told us
some tricks
too, and said
we should try
them out on you.

TRICKY TRICKS TO FIRE UP FIERY FIONA

- Make some tasty-looking biscuits, but sneak in some raisins. Offer one to Fiona and tell her that it's a chocolate chip cookie.

- Dare Fiona to fold a piece of paper up eight times. This will drive her crazy – because it's impossible.

- Say 'hippity hop' after anything you say to Fiona for ten minutes.

FIERY FIONA: Henry is so ANNOYING!

- Repeat everything Fiona says and copy all her actions. This is guaranteed to drive anyone mad – but especially Fiery Fiona.

- Take two eggs – one raw and the other hard-boiled, but keep that a secret. Tell Fiona you can make an egg stand on its rounded end and spin it like a top, but you bet that she can't. Give her the raw egg and watch her fail, while you show off with the hard-boiled egg. Ha!

- Dare Fiona to crumple up a double page of a newspaper, using only one hand. She won't be able to do it – and she'll get very angry trying!

- Make two pin pricks opposite each other near the bottom of a straw. Do the same at the top of the straw too. Give Fiona the straw with a glass of her favourite drink, and watch her struggle to slurp it up. The holes make it almost impossible for the drink to reach the top of the straw.

FIERY FIONA: AAAGH! I'm going straight round to tell Henry exactly what I think of him.

SINGING SORAYA SHRIEKS

SINGING SORAYA: I know some jokes and dares. Would you like to hear them?

As long as she doesn't sing... Go on then, let's hear them.

SINGING SORAYA'S JOKES

How do you mend a tuba?
With a tuba glue.

What sort of music scares balloons?
Pop music!

Why did the girl sit on the ladder to sing?
She wanted to reach the high notes!

What musical key do cows sing in?
Beef flat.

*Why did the man keep his trumpet
in the fridge?*
Because he liked cool music!

SINGING SORAYA'S DARES

- Stand on one foot and sing a song. But as soon as you're back on two feet, you have to stop singing.

- Try singing while you're doing the following:
  1. Holding a cup of water on top of your head and hopping.
  2. Balancing a spoon on your nose.
  3. Licking your elbow.

SOUR SUSAN: Even Soraya won't be able to sing very much if she's doing those dares!

- Eat a mouthful of crackers and then try to whistle.

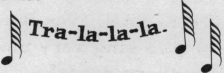

I've got a dare for you, Soraya. Go over to the Purple Hand camp and sing as LOUDLY as you can. With all that racket – sorry, lovely singing – the boys won't be able to think of any good dares, tricks or jokes. And you can be my Second in Command in the Secret Club.

SINGING SORAYA: If my singing will help the girls and the Secret Club, I'll do it.

Tra-la-la-la.

THE WORM

PERFECT PETER: Please will you let me in your club? I'll tell you some really funny jokes.

PERFECT PETER'S JOKES

Patient: Doctor, Doctor, I keep thinking I'm invisible.
   Doctor: Who said that?

What's the best way to catch a rabbit?
Hide in the bushes and make a noise like lettuce.

Where do carrots eat their dinner?
At the veggie-table.

What's green and goes 'boing, boing'?
A spring onion.

**Terrible! I've got a better joke
than those.**

*How do you tell which end of a worm
is the head?*
Tickle him in the middle and watch
where he smiles.

**PERFECT PETER: Please, please
will you let me in your club? I've
got some good dares too.**

PERFECT PETER'S DARES

• Build a tower out of anything you can
find until it is taller than you are.

- On your mum or dad's birthday, wrap yourself up as a birthday present.

That's terrible. Don't tell me any more.

PERFECT PETER: Please, please, please, let me in the club. You haven't even heard my secret yet.

Not now. Go back to
Henry's book and
stay there.

NEW NICK: I've brought you
some flowers, Margaret. I hope
you like them.

PERFECT PETER:
That's the
secret. There's
a w...

MOODY
MARGARET: Ooh,
thank you.

PERFECT PETER: Watch out! That's what I was trying to tell you. There's a w...

AAAAAGH!! Why didn't you tell me? Peter, you're a useless spy. Go home!

THE SECRET CLUB VERSUS THE PURPLE HAND

HORRID HENRY: Your silly Secret Club will never beat the Purple Hand with *those* useless dares and jokes.

Girls are cool and boys drool.

HORRID HENRY: We don't need a stupid rhyme like that to tell us boys are the best and girls are boring – nah nah ne nah nah!

Do some of my dares then. I dare you to sleep in a haunted bedroom.

HORRID HENRY: Easy-peasy. I dare you to hide under someone's bed and pretend to be a ghost by poking their mattress and twitching the duvet.

Okay, I'll do it to you! You'll

be screaming like a big baby. Here are some dares for your silly friends too.

DIZZY DAVE has to keep still for one whole hour.

BABBLING BOB has to keep quiet for one whole hour.

ANXIOUS ANDREW has to sing in public for thirty seconds.

RUDE RALPH has to stand up every time Miss Battle-Axe enters the room, and call her 'Your Majesty'.

TOUGH TOBY has to go to school in his sister's nightie.

Why did Greedy Graham eat his homework?
The teacher told him it was a piece of cake.

   Why did Beefy Bert eat a £1 coin?
His mum told him it was for his dinner.

Mum: Do you like your new teacher?
Horrid Henry: No. She told me to sit at the front of the class for the present, and then she didn't give me one.

HORRID HENRY: Don't listen to that misery guts and her stupid friends. My book's better – read it and see!

That's got rid of him and all the
other stinky boys. The Secret
Club rules and my book is the
best ever. Read on for the official
top-secret results ...

Top Secret Results

	SECRET CLUB	PURPLE HAND
DARES/TRICKS	100	-500
JOKES	100	-750

RESULT: The Secret Club wins!
The Purple Hand loses! Now it's your turn to award points for the dares, tricks and jokes in this book:

DARES/TRICKS	...../10
JOKES	...../10
GRAND TOTAL	...../20

When you've read *Horrid Henry's Double Dare*, fill in your score for that book too. Which book came out on top?

HORRID HENRY'S DOUBLE DARE	...../20
MOODY MARGARET STRIKES BACK	...../20

HORRiD HENRY BOOKS

Horrid Henry
Horrid Henry and the Secret Club
Horrid Henry Tricks the Tooth Fairy
Horrid Henry's Nits
Horrid Henry Gets Rich Quick
Horrid Henry's Haunted House
Horrid Henry and the Mummy's Curse
Horrid Henry's Revenge
Horrid Henry and the Bogey Babysitter
Horrid Henry's Stinkbomb
Horrid Henry's Underpants
Horrid Henry Meets the Queen
Horrid Henry and the Mega-Mean Time Machine
Horrid Henry and the Football Fiend
Horrid Henry's Christmas Cracker
Horrid Henry and the Abominable Snowman
Horrid Henry Robs the Bank

Horrid Henry's Big Bad Book
Horrid Henry's Wicked Ways
Horrid Henry's Evil Enemies
Horrid Henry Rules the World
Horrid Henry's House of Horrors

Horrid Henry's Joke Book
Horrid Henry's Jolly Joke Book
Horrid Henry's Mighty Joke Book

Once you've read all the Horrid Henry books,
why not see how well you know Henry and friends
and try the activity and puzzle books:

Horrid Henry's Brainbusters
Horrid Henry's Headscratchers
Horrid Henry's Mindbenders
Horrid Henry's Colouring Book
Horrid Henry's Puzzle Book
Horrid Henry's Sticker Book
Horrid Henry's Mad Mazes
Horrid Henry's Wicked Wordsearches
Horrid Henry's Crazy Crosswords

Visit Horrid Henry's website at
www.horridhenry.co.uk for competitions, games,
downloads and a monthly newsletter!